The Big Book Adventure

Emily Ford
& Tim Warnes

BOOK CLUB

OPEN

Book Club

Every day
10–4pm

Join our club!

You'll never guess where I have been,
Or who I've met or what I've seen.
Shall I tell you?

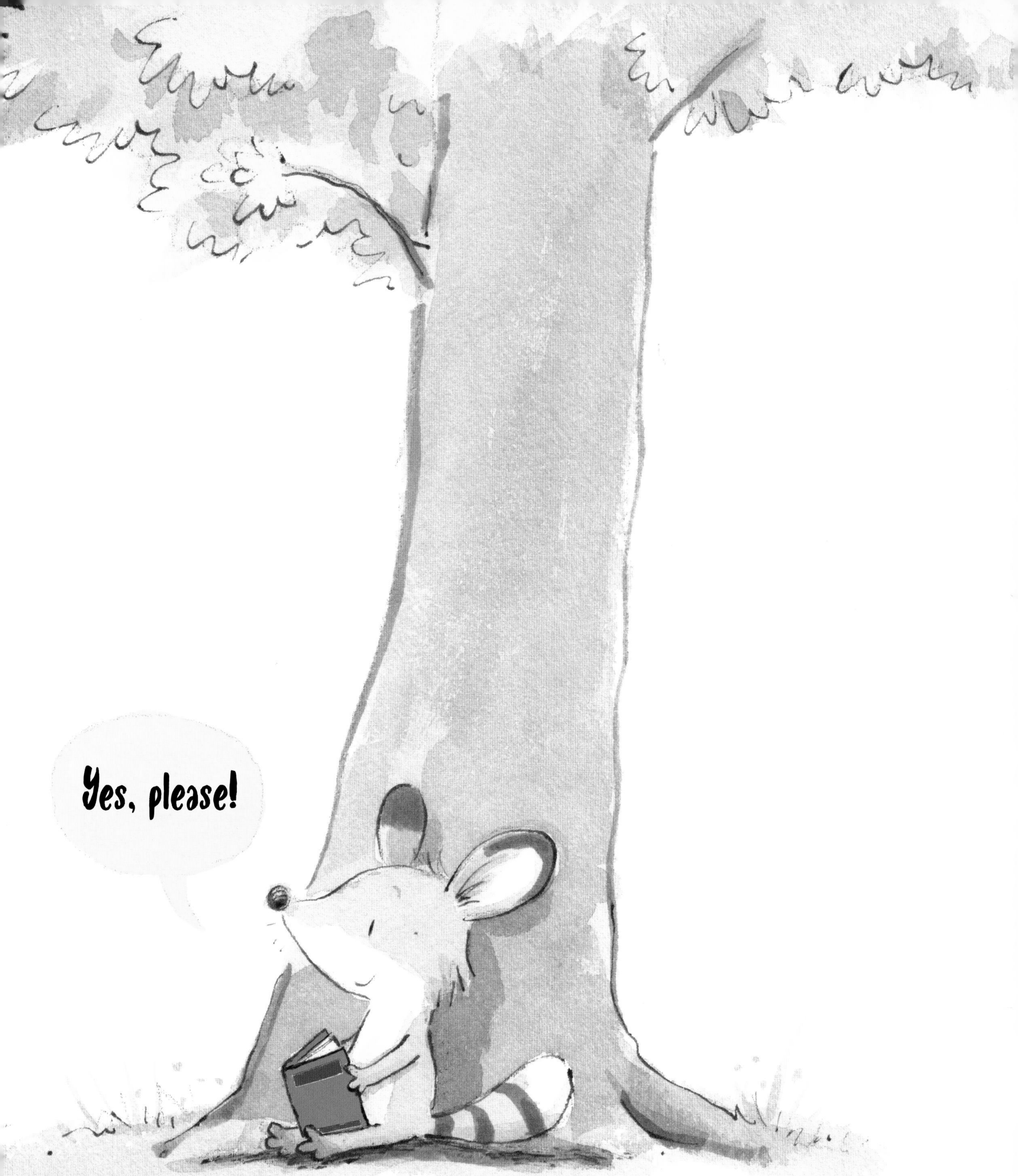
Yes, please!

Well, first I found a little door,
Right there on a tree.
I stepped inside and made some friends
And joined them all for tea.

Next, I met a mermaid
And we both went for a swim.
Then she sat and brushed her hair
While I listened to her sing.

THEN OFF TO GRAN'S WENT RED AND I—
SHE WORE HER BRIGHT RED HOOD.
I'M SURE I SAW A BUSHY TAIL
AS WE RAN THROUGH THE WOOD.

After that, I found some gold,
On an island out at sea.
A chest of gleaming coins and jewels,
All waiting there for me!

Well, you'll never guess where I have been.
Or who I've met, or what I've seen.
Shall I tell **you?**

Yes, please!

First I met a fairy
Who cast a special spell.
This tiny fairy flicked her wand
Now I can fly as well!

GALACTIC RACE

U.S.A.
$1.00

★ ★ ★

NO. 358
APRIL

Then I built a giant rocket,
And flew to outer space.
I joined in the galactic race
And finished in first place!

Cool!

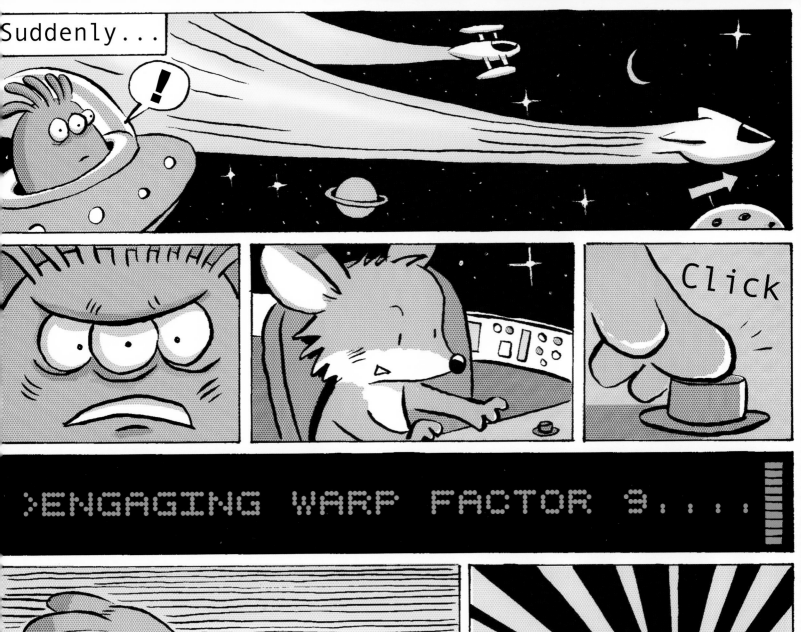

And after lunch a dragon came
And took me for a spin.
He liked to roar and breathe hot flames
But I'm NOT afraid of him!

Then walking home, I saw a house,
And stopped there for a snack.
The bears who lived there seemed quite mad
So I won't be going back.

Then suddenly the carpet came—
I've never been so high!
And you were with me, by my side,
As stars lit up the sky.

Your day sounds **amazing!**

And your day sounds **great** too!

I'd love to see
The things you've seen. . .

Then I know what we should do!

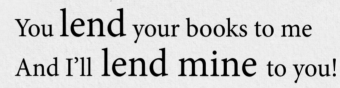

You **lend** your books to me
And I'll **lend mine** to you!

Now we're happy as can be,
So let's go **read** beneath **our tree**.

The End